BRICK WALL
TRAFFIC CONE
7
8.2
1.1
1.2
.3
WHEELBARROW
.5
PICKAX
HARD...
HAT
SHOVEL
.3
.8
4.3
4.1
1.1
REAR VIEW
14.5
LATTICE
DAISY

For Matt.
Because he can lift the heavy stuff.

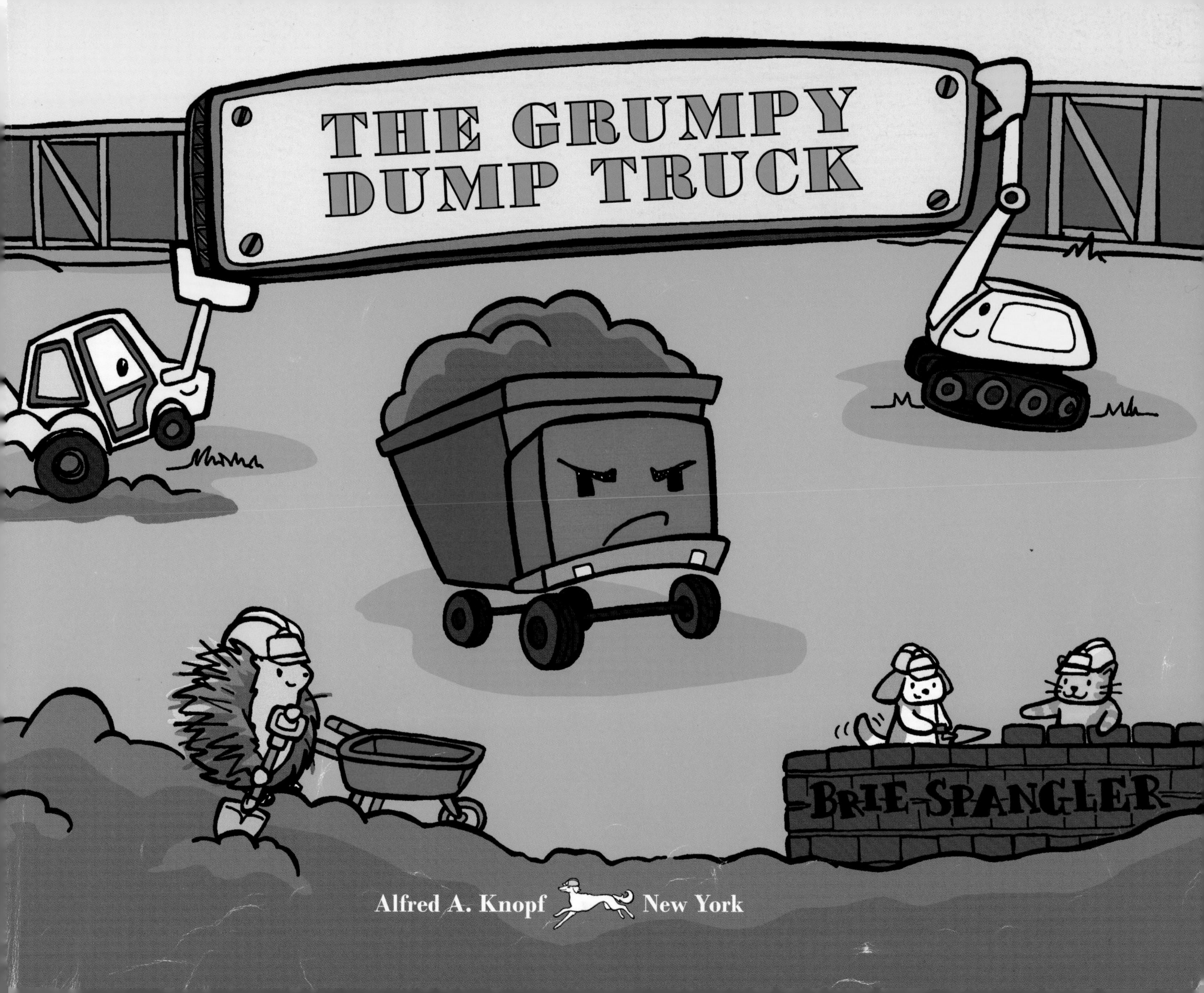
THE GRUMPY DUMP TRUCK
BRIE SPANGLER
Alfred A. Knopf New York

THIS IS A BORZOI BOOK PUBLISHED BY ALFRED A. KNOPF

Visit us on the Web! www.randomhouse.com/kids

Educators and librarians, for a variety of teaching tools, visit us at www.randomhouse.com/teachers

Library of Congress Cataloging-in-Publication Data
Spangler, Brie.
The grumpy dump truck / Brie Spangler. — 1st ed.
p. cm.
Summary: Bertrand the dump truck is always grumpy and mean, but a chance encounter with a porcupine reveals that his bad mood has a cause.
ISBN 978-0-375-85839-0 (trade) — ISBN 978-0-375-95839-7 (lib. bdg.)
[1. Mood (Psychology)—Fiction. 2. Dump trucks—Fiction. 3. Porcupines—Fiction. 4. Construction equipment—Fiction.] I. Title.
PZ7.S7365Gru 2009
[E]—dc22
2008024528

The illustrations in this book were created digitally.

MANUFACTURED IN MALAYSIA
July 2009
10 9 8 7 6 5 4 3 2 1
First Edition

Random House Children's Books supports the First Amendment and celebrates the right to read.

Once there was a dump truck.

And while he was good at his job . . .

Morning, Joe.
Morning, Tilly.
We need more mortar.

. . . his attitude was rather

CRABBY
It's too sunny and hot out to do all this work!
And above all,
GRUMPY
Everything is the PITS!

He was rude to the backhoe.

And he was a real pain to the crane.

He shouted at the foreman.

And he honked at the bricklayers.

One day, while Bertrand was doing his usual grumbling . . .

La-La-La!

. . . he ran into a problem.

EEK!
POKE!
shoot!
pow!
ping!
zing!
zoom!

Bertrand was furious.

TILLY!!
Good gravy!
You almost gave me a flat tire!
I'm sorry, Bertrand.

Tilly tried to explain herself . . .

. . . but Bertrand was still upset.

Tilly tried again . . .

. . . but Bertrand wasn't convinced.

Tilly climbed up on a cinder block . . .

. . . and gently plucked out the quill.

But to her surprise, she found more than a quill in Bertrand's tire.

Oh, OWIE-OW!

I can't believe you did that!

Tilly found a . . .

No wonder you were so grumpy.

Suddenly Bertrand felt much better.

And for the first time, he said,

THANK YOU.
You're welcome.

Bertrand wasn't so grumpy anymore.

That's great!
Come with me, I have just the thing.

You can help us in our garden!

This is fun!

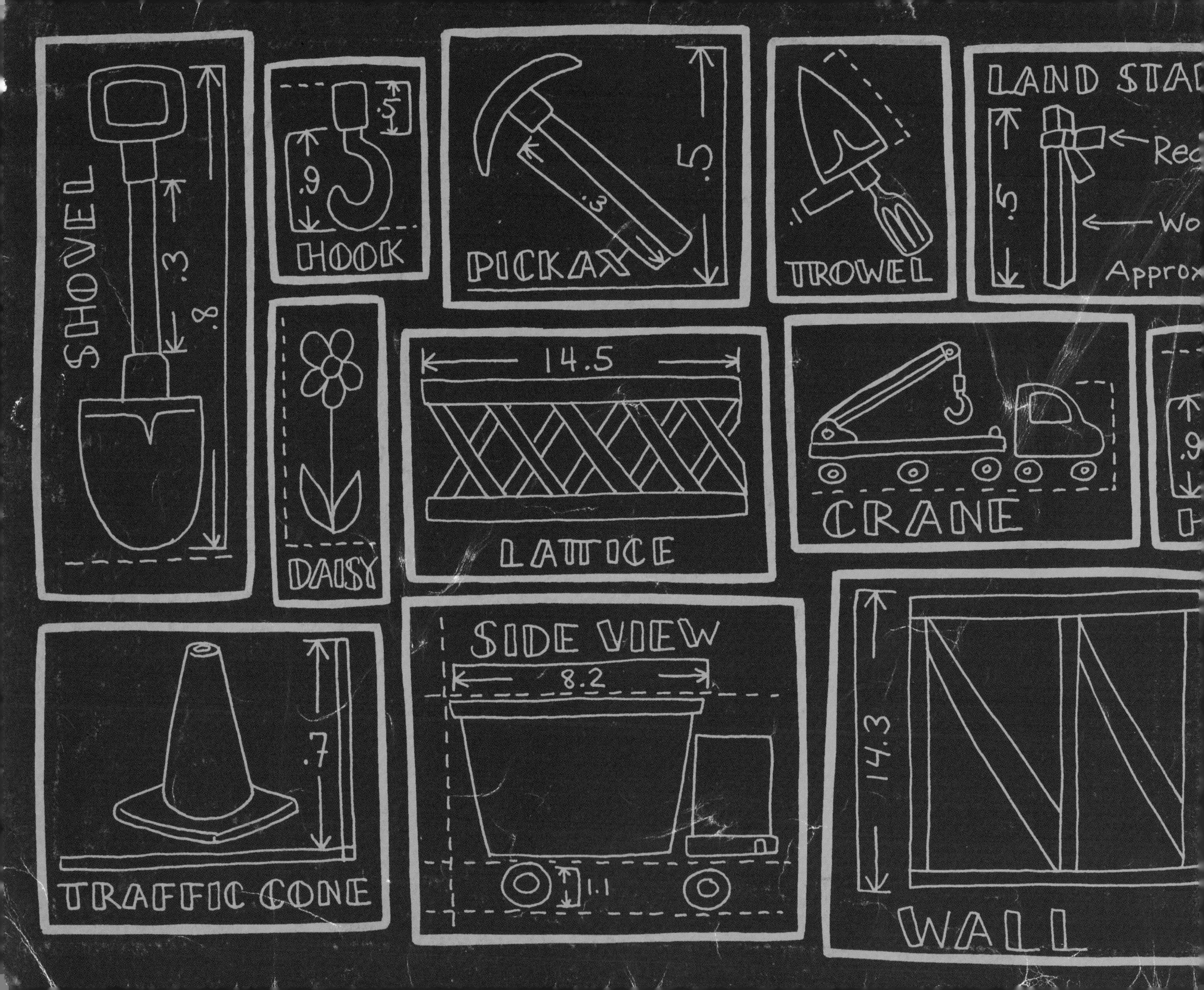
SHOVEL
.8
.3
HOOK
.5
.9
PICKAX
.3
5
TROWEL
.1
LAND
.5
DAISY
14.5
LATTICE
CRANE
.9
TRAFFIC CONE
.7
SIDE VIEW
8.2
1.1
14.3
WALL